## A NOTE TO PARENTS

When your children are ready to "step into reading," giving them the right books is as crucial as giving them the right food to eat. **Step into Reading Books** present exciting stories and information reinforced with lively, colorful illustrations that make learning to read fun, satisfying, and worthwhile. They are priced so that acquiring an entire library of them is affordable. And they are beginning readers with a difference—they're written on five levels.

**Early Step into Reading Books** are designed for brand-new readers, with large type and only one or two lines of very simple text per page. **Step 1 Books** feature the same easy-to-read type as the Early Step into Reading Books, but with more words per page. **Step 2 Books** are both longer and slightly more difficult, while **Step 3 Books** introduce readers to paragraphs and fully developed plot lines. **Step 4 Books** offer exciting nonfiction for the increasingly independent reader.

www.randomhouse.com/kids
www.berenstainbears.com

*Library of Congress Cataloging-in-Publication Data:*
Berenstain, Stan, 1923–
The Berenstain Bears catch the bus / by Stan & Jan Berenstain.
p. cm. — (Step into reading. Step 1 book.)
Summary: As the minutes pass and the school bus gets closer to their house, Brother and Sister are in increasing danger of missing it.
ISBN 0-679-89227-3 (trade). — ISBN 0-679-99227-8 (lib. bdg.)
[1. Bears—Fiction. 2. Time—Fiction. 3. Punctuality—Fiction. 4. Stories in rhyme.] I. Berenstain, Jan, 1923–   . II. Title. III. Series.
PZ8.3.B4493Bgv 1999
[E]—dc21  98-29760

Printed in the United States of America  10 9 8 7 6 5 4 3 2 1

Step into Reading®

# The Berenstain Bears

## CATCH THE BUS

Stan & Jan Berenstain

A Step 1 Book

Random House 🏠 New York

**6:59**

It is almost seven,
as you can see.
All is quiet
in the Bears'
Home Sweet Tree.

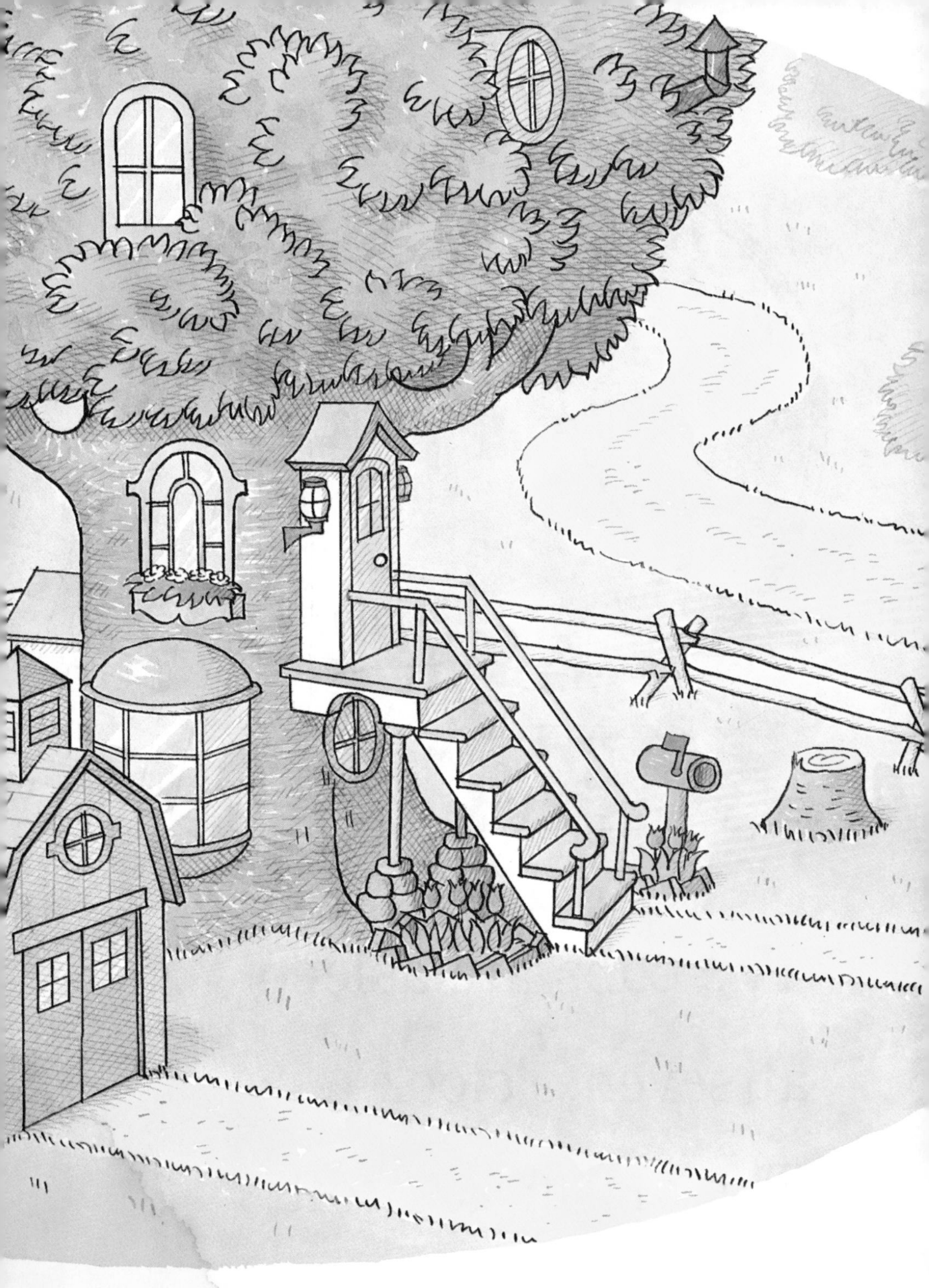

**7:00**

The cubs are asleep
at seven o'clock.
The alarm goes off.
It is quite a shock.

Five minutes later,
they are back to sleep.
Brother and Sister
are back to sleep!

**7:10**

Papa's coffee
starts to perk.
Papa will soon
be going to work.

And off to work
goes Grizzly Gus,
the driver of
the cubs' school bus.

7:20

The school bus starts

on its way

to pick up cubs

for school today.

**7:25**

What about Brother
and Sister Bear?
Will they be ready
when Gus gets there?

**7:30**

The bus stops here.

The bus stops there.

It picks up bear

after bear after bear.

Will our cubs be ready?

It is a worry.

They may not be—

unless they hurry.

7:35

But are <u>they</u> worrying?

They are not.

Are they hurrying?

They are not.

7:40

BEAR
SCHOO

Gus picks up Bob
and Liz and Fred.
<u>Are</u> Brother and Sister
<u>still in bed?</u>

22

7:45

Ma sees the bus.

She starts to worry.

To catch that bus,

her cubs must hurry.

But upstairs there is not
a single sound—
the cubs are not even
up and around!

No more dreams
for Sister and Brother.
They wake up to
an angry mother.

The old school bus is
almost there—
at the house of
Brother and Sister Bear!

7:50

7:55

**7:56**

Hurry! Hurry!

Rush! Rush! Rush!

**7:57**

Wash and dress.

Comb and brush.

**7:58**

Downstairs! Downstairs in a flash!

**7:59**

Eat some breakfast!

Off you dash!

At eight o'clock,
they catch the bus
and say hello
to Grizzly Gus!

Moral:

If you sleep past seven,

you might be late

when the school bus comes

for you at eight!